The Tric of Fringle

Written by Jo Windsor
Illustrated by Alan Cochrane

Rigby

In Moontide Mountains, Fringle Village lies contentedly in the midday sun. It's festival time and the villagers are busy preparing for the town's 100th Anniversary.

NEXT DAY... the trouble starts when BAS and JUPITER hit town!

They take little time to create havoc...

I don't know what to do!

SUPANOVA café

OO-OOPS!!

OH! So sorry!

5

Oh dear! I don't know what to do!

Thanks for the food!

Through the townsfolks' backyards, side streets, and highways, Bas and Jupiter create more havoc before anyone can stop them.

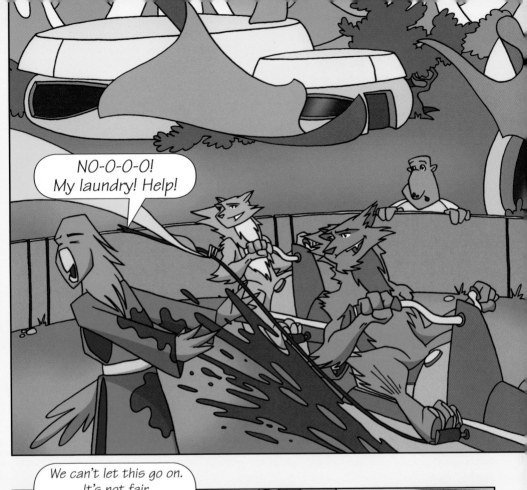

CALL A SECRET MEETING! CALL A SECRET MEETING!

Yes. A meeting.

LATER THAT NIGHT, as darkness covers the Blue Forest, the village of Fringle sleeps. All is quiet – except for whispering voices in a glade in the nearby forest.

Good of you all to come.

We need a plan to outsmart those two cattoos so they can't ruin our celebrations.

The meeting goes long into the night and the moon is high in the sky when it finally breaks up. But a plan to outsmart the cattoos is put together with everyone taking part...

PLAN TO OUTSMART CATTOOS

1: Tell them they can have anything.

2: Invite them to the celebrations.

3: Tell them they can cut the festival cake.

4: Put a secret compartment in the cake and fill it with Buzzalips.

Look, what will it take to get you to behave? We'll give you anything... anything!

Anything? That's a big word.

Anything? Okay... Let's see...

How... how about being special guests at the Anniversary Day?

That... would be... good.

You could cut the Anniversary Cake...

Yes... YES! CUT THE CAKE!

Anniversary Day dawns bright and sunny! Everyone is out on the streets — smiling, laughing, happy. A band strikes up and the Mayoral Parade, surrounded by cheering villagers, makes its way slowly toward the stage.

13

A blast from a horn, and the noise and merrymaking begins to subside. Everyone takes their seats. All eyes turn toward the stage as the mayor steps up to the podium.

To all the people of Fringle Village! Welcome to our special day! Today, we celebrate 100 years of living in the Moontide Mountains.

We are asking guest cattoos, Bas and Jupiter, to cut the Anniversary Cake. And so...

...BRING OUT THE CAKE!

THE CAKE! THE CAKE! BRING OUT THE CAKE!

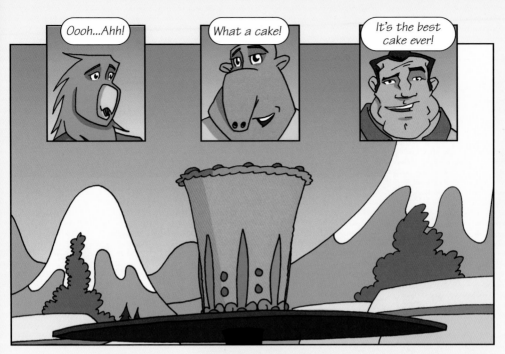

Then, from out of the cake, swarm hundreds of BUZZALIPS!

16

THE COMIC

The comic uses an arrangement of pictures and words to tell a story.

The reader follows the storyline frame by frame through:
narrative panels
picture information
speech and thought bubbles

HOW TO WRITE A COMIC

Step One   Think of a story that has: | Plot | Characters | Setting |

Step Two   Plan your story.

Introduction

| Who |
| Where |
| When |

→ | Event |
| Event |
| Event |

→ | Problem | →

| Event |
| Event |

→ | Resolution |

Step Three   Look at your plan.
Put your introduction into
a narrative panel.

Step Four

Plan your comic frame by frame. Think about the reading sequence and how the storyline tracks from frame to frame.

Reading Track

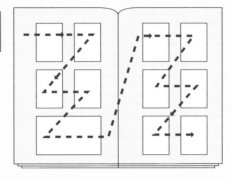

Think about the text frames as a stage for action.

Will the picture and text need a big or small frame? Will there be narrative panels, speech bubbles, thought bubbles, or illustrative text?

LATER THAT NIGHT, as darkness covers the Blue Forest, the village of Fringle sleeps. All is quiet – except for whispering voices in a glade in the nearby forest.

Narrative Panel

Oh dear! I don't know what to do!

Thought Bubble

Thanks for the food!

Speech Bubble

Step Five

Check your comic.
Is the storyline easy to follow?

Guide Notes

Title: **The Tricksters of Fringle**
Stage: Fluency (4)

Text Form: Comic
Approach: Guided Reading
Processes: Thinking Critically, Exploring Language, Processing Information
Written and Visual Focus: Comic, Speech Bubbles, Thought Bubbles, Phonetic
Representations

THINKING CRITICALLY
(sample questions)
- What type of narrative story is *The Tricksters of Fringle*?
- Why do you think Bas and Jupiter want to cause havoc?
- Why do you think it is necessary to have a plan to outsmart the cattoos?
- Do you think the action that the villagers took was good? Why/Why not?

EXPLORING LANGUAGE

Terminology
Spread, author, illustrator, credits, imprint information, ISBN number

Vocabulary
Clarify: contentedly, settlement, celebration, unbeknown, glade, podium, subside, havoc
Pronouns: you, we, it
Adjectives: *whispering* voices, *mayoral* parade, *anniversary* cake
Homonym: wait/weight
Antonyms: after/before, sunny/rainy
Synonyms: annoy/pester, contentedly/happily

Print Conventions
Dash, semi-colon, hyphen: OO-OOPS!
Apostrophe – possessive (townsfolks' backyards, town's 100th Anniversary, villagers' plans)